Where Has the Moon Gone?

by Hiroyuki Arai • illustrated by Yukiko Kobayashi

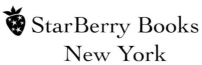 StarBerry Books
New York

Publisher's Cataloging-in-Publication Data
Names: Arai, Hiroyuki, author. | Kobayashi, Yukiko, illustrator.
Title: Where has the moon gone? / by Hiroyuki Arai ; illustrated by Yukiko Kobayashi.
Description: New York, NY: StarBerry Books, an imprint of Kane Press, Inc., 2018.
Identifiers: ISBN 9781575659701 (Hardcover) | 9781575659718 (ebook) | LCCN 2017953340
Summary: Two mice wonder where the moon goes during the day and decide to search for it.
Subjects: LCSH Mice--Juvenile fiction. | Moon--Juvenile fiction. | Night--Juvenile fiction.
| Imagination--Juvenile fiction. | BISAC JUVENILE FICTION / Imagination & Play
| JUVENILE FICTION / Animals / Mice, Hamsters, Guinea Pigs, etc. | JUVENILE
FICTION / Nature & the Natural World / General
Classification: LCC PZ7.A661 Wh 2018 | DDC [E]--dc23
Library of Congress Control Number: 2017953340

10 9 8 7 6 5 4 3 2 1

First published in English in the United States of America in 2018
by StarBerry Books, an imprint of Kane Press, Inc.
Printed in China
StarBerry Books is a trademark of Kane Press, Inc.
www.kanepress.com

Chuchu and Chichi are two good friends.
They liked to walk together under the inky night sky.
No matter where they went, the moon followed them.
"The moon really likes us," they said to each other.

One day, they began to wonder where the moon goes during the daytime.

"Let's go find it!" said Chuchu.

"Do you think the moon is up in that tree?" asked Chichi.
"Let's climb up and take a look!" said Chuchu.

The two little mice climbed up the tree.
And they found that their "moon" was a
yellow balloon.

They looked into the window next to the tree.
There was something yellow and round inside the house.
"Is that the moon?"
They scampered along a branch and scrambled up to
the window.

They climbed into the house and saw that their "moon" was . . .
a big round fruit.
"Smells good!"
"Let's eat it."

Chuchu and Chichi
bit into the moon-fruit.
It was very tart!

Then they spotted a gleaming yellow ball. It was peeking out from behind a long pink curtain.

"The moon!" said Chichi.

"It's smaller than I thought," said Chuchu.

They ran toward the curtain and pulled it back.

Behind the curtain was an
angry black cat.
The two little mice ran to the
window as fast as they could.
But the cat was fast, too.

The angry cat's claws had almost caught them.
Chichi cried, "Hurry, hurry!"
He grabbed the string of the big balloon and
bit down *HARD*.

The two little mice started to fly.
"Look at the sky!" cried Chuchu.

The moon hung brightly above them.
"Moon! Where have you been?"
"Oh, it's so good to see you again!"